Five Children and IT

Written by Jan L. Coates / Based on characters by Edith Nesbit

CARAMEL TREE

CHAPTER 1

The Children Find Buried Treasure

"Are we there, yet?" Cyril complained. "We've been driving for days."

"Don't exaggerate, Cyril," said his older sister, Anthea.

Cyril made a face at her. "Stuff your nose back in your book."

"Reading makes the time go faster," Anthea replied.

In fact, they had been driving for close to three hours. The first hour was spent in traffic driving out of the city, where they lived, the second hour on the highway, and the third hour driving along winding country lanes.

Finally, as the driver turned a corner, Mom exclaimed, "There it is. Your home for the summer!"

A long gravel driveway lined with maple trees led them past a big red barn, up to a large white house with fancy woodwork and dark green shutters. A wide porch wrapped itself around the front and both sides of the house.

"Oh, Mom," Anthea said. "It's just like Green Gables."

"Does Anne Shirley live here?" Jane asked dreamily.

"Who's Anne Shirley?" Cyril interrupted.

"She's the girl in the book I am reading," Anthea said.

"Well, that's dumb." Robert jumped into the conversation. "How can a stupid book character live here?"

Mom laughed. "No, Anne Shirley does not live here. But I hope you'll be able to grow your imagination as big as Anne's while you're here!"

The children climbed out of the van and pulled their suitcases up onto the porch of their summer vacation home.

Most of the year, the five children lived in the city. A great mass of skyscrapers, rumbling subway cars, noisy trucks and millions of busy people. As you know, cities are lovely places, especially if you have money to spend, but city children don't need to make up their own games – cities have everything organized for you; theaters, soccer clubs, hockey teams, dance lessons and school.

"Did you bring your laptop, Cyril?" Robert asked.

Mom laughed again. "No need to bother with technology – there's no Internet service for miles."

"But, can we text our friends?" Jane asked.

Mom shook her head. "No cell phone service either, I'm afraid. I suppose you could call them on the telephone. Otherwise, you'll have to rely on your own brains and imagination to keep yourselves entertained."

"Humph!" Martha, their housekeeper, sneered. "It'll take more than brains and imagination to keep these children out of trouble all summer." She unbuckled The Lamb, who was the

youngest of the five children, from his car seat and carried him into the house. Everybody called him The Lamb because his first words had been "Ba... Ba... a..."

They put their bags in their rooms, then Jane asked, "Can we go exploring, Mom? In the woods behind the house?"

"Certainly, but don't go so far that you can't hear Martha if she calls you. I'll be back in a few days. I need to spend time with Grandma until she's feeling better."

The four older children all kissed their mother goodbye, then set off for the woods.

The squirrels chattered, birds sang and a gentle breeze rustled through the pine branches. Before long, the four children came to a winding open path lined with wildflowers that led down to an enormous sand and gravel pit.

"Wow!" exclaimed Cyril. "There's sure to be buried treasure in a place like this."

"You're exaggerating again, Cyril," Anthea said as she walked ahead.

"It's almost like being at the beach," Jane said.

"Only no water." Robert picked up a stick and started digging in the sand. "We could make a sand castle, though."

Anthea wandered off from the others and sat down on a large rock. As she stared at the sand, all of a sudden she saw something move. A hand! A monkey hand!

"Quickly!" she shouted. "There's something here!"

By the time the others arrived, the hand had disappeared. "Right there," Anthea said, pointing to the spot. "I saw a hand – a monkey hand, I'm sure."

They all got down on their hands and knees and started to dig.

"There it is!" Jane shouted. "Grab it!"

Cyril caught two fingers of the furry hand and held on tight.

"Be gentle. Is it a monkey?" Anthea said. "A sand monkey?"

"It looks like E.T.," Jane said. "Maybe it's an alien!"

"I wish IT would come out of the sand," Cyril said. He pulled on the tiny furry hand. But almost immediately, he fell back as the creature popped out of the hole.

The children gasped.

CHAPTER 2

The Children Have a Taste of Fame

The creature stood up, shook the sand off its fur and glared up at the children.

"Please do not insult me. I don't know what an alien is, but I am no monkey. I am a Psammead." (His name is spelled like that, but it is pronounced like this: SammyAdd, in case you're confused by the "P".)

"B...b... but what are you, then?" Anthea asked.

The creature stood up as tall as he could which was not very tall at all. He had the hands and feet of a monkey, a perfectly round furry belly, ears like an elf and the hairy wrinkled face of a very old man. A caveman, perhaps. He had large brown eyes, and on top of his head, two extra eyes on long stalks, like a snail. "I am a Sand Fairy," he announced proudly. "And I am as old as time itself."

"Are you a caveman, then?" Robert asked.

The Sand Fairy glared at him. "I am much more refined than an ordinary caveman. But I once granted wishes to cavemen, back a few thousand years ago. They asked for things like a nice T-Rex steak for supper, or perhaps an Ichthyosaurus, if they were more in the mood for fish." He stretched his skinny arms out and yawned. "Come to think of it, I believe I've been asleep for a very long time." He looked all around, then laughed. "I've never seen people wearing so many clothes."

"Do you still grant wishes?" Jane asked.

The Psammead rubbed his round belly, and then scratched his furry head. "I just did," he said, turning to Cyril, who was still lying on the ground. "When you wished I would come out of the sand."

"Can you grant us another wish?" Anthea asked.

"I suppose so. But it's exhausting work. Don't wish for anything too difficult."

"Please excuse us for one minute," Anthea said.

The four children walked away and stood under a tree. "We need to wish for something we all want," Anthea said.

"I'd like to be famous," Robert said. "A famous hockey player."

Jane clapped her hands. "Yes, and I could be a princess." She turned to Anthea. "Who would you like to be, Anthea?"

Anthea straightened up and flipped her hair back behind her. "I'd like to be a Hollywood actress."

"And I'd like to be a pop star." Cyril held his arms out and pretended he was playing a guitar.

They returned to find the Sand Fairy had fallen asleep.

Anthea gently poked his shoulder. "Excuse me," she whispered into one hairy ear. "We're ready now."

He jumped up and rubbed his eyes. "Well, what will it be, then?"

"We'd like to be famous," she said. "If that's okay with you."

The Sand Fairy groaned then blew up like a balloon. His snail eyes spun in circles, and then he collapsed to the ground and began burrowing back into the sand. "Oh, just one thing I forgot to mention," he said. "Your wish will disappear at sunset. Goodbye!"

The children looked around at each other and laughed. "Martha will never recognize us," Jane said. Her hair was long and straight, rather than short and curly. She was dressed in a puffy white princess gown, with matching heels.

"Where's your castle?" Anthea asked.

"This gear's a little hot for a sunny day," Robert said. He lifted up the face mask on his hockey helmet and turned to show them the number 87 on his back.

"Just call me Mr. Cool," Cyril sang. He started to dance and was surprised at how smoothly his feet moved.

"Then, who am I?" Anthea asked. She was holding an

expensive leather handbag and wearing big heart-shaped sunglasses.

"You're a famous Hollywood actress!" Jane exclaimed.

"You're so stylish, Anthea! I wonder what movies you're in."

"Let's go back to the house, and see if Martha recognizes us," Cyril suggested.

Before they left, Anthea made a circle of stones around the area where the Sand Fairy had disappeared.

"These shoes are really uncomfortable," Jane complained as they walked.

"Try walking in skates!" Robert answered.

But when they got to the house, Martha refused to let them in. "I don't know you children, at all. We don't allow strangers in the house."

The children were very hungry, but they could not convince Martha that they were really Robert, Anthea, Cyril and Jane.

"How do you know their names? Did they put you up to this?"

Martha asked the famous children. "Well, you can tell them to come home at once. They're late for lunch." And with that, Martha slammed the door.

The children laughed and went to sit on the picnic table out front.

"Look!" Robert pointed to the road. "It's a traffic jam."

"Out here? In the middle of the country?" Anthea said.

Hundreds of cars and vans were driving up the road toward the white house. They pulled over to the side of the road, then hundreds of people carrying microphones, television cameras and notebooks, ran towards the four children.

"They're news reporters!" Anthea said. "How did they find us?"

"It's their job to spy on famous people," Cyril said. "Find out everything about their private lives and get them in trouble. Just so the media can make money."

The reporters ran towards the famous children like a pack of wild dogs. They pushed and shoved as they tried to get closer to the children. Cameras flashed brightly as the reporters stretched out with their microphones and asked very personal questions.

Jane hid behind Anthea. "I'm scared," she whispered. "Why are they being so nosy?"

"Quick, let's hide in the barn," Robert said.

The children ran toward the barn. The crowd chased after them, shouting and shoving.

"Lock the door!" Robert yelled. "They're crazy!"

The four children huddled together in a corner and listened to the banging and screaming. The barn door shook as the crowd pushed against it. "I don't want to be famous anymore," Jane said, crying into Anthea's shoulder.

"Why don't they just mind their own business?" Robert said.

Cyril looked at his watch. "It's almost time for the sun to set. Here, let's hide in this haystack."

When the reporters finally broke the door down, they found only four ordinary children playing hide-and-seek in the hay.

"What do you mean, famous superstars?" Robert said.

"We don't know anybody famous. Now, please leave us alone. This is *private* property."

Martha had supper waiting for them when they returned to the house. "Why did you children try to trick me by sending those strangers to the door?" She shook her head. "There's even more noisy traffic here in the country than in the city. I thought we came here for a bit of peace and quiet," she said. "And why didn't you come in for lunch?"

"We couldn't," Anthea explained. "We were held back by THEM. Now, please can we have our supper? We are starving."

"Okay, and then straight to bed, all of you. I don't want you making any more noise and disturbing The Lamb." Martha picked up the baby and took him to his room.

CHAPTER **3**

The Children Get Rich (Sort of)!

The children all slept very deeply that night. In the morning, they met in the upstairs hall. "Did you dream about a Sand Fairy?" Jane asked.

They all smiled at each other and nodded.

"That was no dream," Cyril said. "The Psammead is real. And I was a pop star... for a while. And I am not exaggerating!"

"Yes, Cyril." Anthea smiled. "Even though that wish didn't work out very well, let's go see him again, right after breakfast."

"Let's take a shovel this time," Robert suggested.

They easily found the circle of stones and began digging. The Sand Fairy grumbled, then stood up and shook himself off. "Well, what is it now?" he asked.

"Please, sir. Could you arrange it so that Martha won't notice the gifts you give us? It would be ever so much easier," Anthea said.

"And, we have another wish," Cyril said. "We would like to be incredibly rich, if that's possible, I mean."

"Greedy little things, aren't you?" The Sand Fairy shook his head. "I'll try, but granting two wishes at the same time is extremely difficult." He closed his eyes and blew himself up as big as a small hot air balloon, then collapsed back to the ground.

"Oh!" Jane exclaimed, looking around. "My eyes!"

The sand pit was full of shiny silver coins. Robert picked one up. "Silver dollars!" he said.

"Thousands and millions of silver dollars!" Cyril shouted. "We're rich!"

They all bent down and began stuffing the coins into their pockets.

"They're very heavy, aren't they?" Jane said as they made their way up the path. "How far is it to town?"

"A mile or two, I'd guess," Cyril said. "I'm going to buy a car."

"But you're not old enough to drive," Anthea said.

"I'll save it for when I am."

They went to the candy store first. "Could we please have a hundred dollars' worth of mixed candy?" Robert asked.

The clerk looked at the handfuls of silver dollars. "And where did you get that funny money? We only take paper money, debit and credit cards."

"But they're real silver dollars," Cyril insisted.

"Then take them to the bank. I'm not interested in filling up my cash register with that heavy old stuff. Good day!"

The children went across the street to the bank.

"We'd like to open a bank account," Anthea said to the man

behind the counter. "We need a place to keep our money and a debit card." All the children dumped their pockets full of silver dollars onto the counter.

The bank teller looked at them strangely. "Yes... well... just let me make a phone call," he said.

A few minutes later, the door burst open and two policemen, followed by an elderly man, raced into the bank.

"Is this your stolen collection, Mr. Wilson?" one officer said to the elderly man.

Mr. Wilson picked up several of the coins. "Some of them could be, but it would take me days to look through all of these coins."

"They're our coins," Cyril said. "We... um... we found them in the sand pit out by our summer house."

The policeman looked sternly at the children. "Don't leave town. We may need to ask you more questions."

"Yes, sir," Anthea said.

"I'm hungry," Robert said when they got back outside. He dug around in his sock, then held up a five-dollar bill he had saved from his allowance. "Maybe that hotdog vendor will sell us four hotdogs."

"Mustard and ketchup on your hotdogs?" the vendor asked.

"Oh, yes, please," all the children said.

They ate their snack as they walked home. They passed the sand pit just as the sun was sinking.

"It's not shiny anymore," Jane said sadly. "It's only sand."

Cyril laughed. "Imagine the look on Mr. Wilson's face when he finds a big pile of sand instead of shiny silver coins on his desk."

"At least the police won't have any more questions for us!" Anthea said.

"But it's another wasted wish," Robert complained. "I'm starting to wonder if that Sand Fairy isn't granting his own wishes, too."

"Yes," Anthea said. "I wonder if he's wishing that our wishes will all go horribly wrong. We haven't had anything good happen yet."

"Maybe tomorrow," Cyril said.

CHAPTER 4

The Lamb
Is Too Popular

"You children will have to look after The Lamb for me this morning," Martha said the next day. "I've got heaps of laundry to do."

"Do we have to?" Robert protested.

Anthea picked up The Lamb. "He is getting awfully heavy to carry around," she said as they walked to the sand pit. "Although, of course we all love him, don't we?"

The other three grumbled, but finally agreed with her.

"Let's ask for something useful, today," Jane suggested.

"How about we each ask for just $1,000?" Cyril said.

"That's still a lot of money, but we must ask for it in paper money," Anthea said.

It was difficult to find the Sand Fairy as the coins had prevented them from putting the ring of stones around his hole the day before. After an hour, they gave up and walked up the path out of the sand pit. Robert was carrying The Lamb. "He's so heavy," he complained. "I wish somebody else would want him so we wouldn't have to look after him all the time."

If the children had looked behind, they would have seen the Sand Fairy's ears twitching. He had heard Robert's wish.

As the children waited to cross the road, a red sports car screeched to a stop. A fancy lady wearing lots of jewelry stepped out of the car and came straight to The Lamb. "I love that baby!" she announced. Without even asking, she grabbed The Lamb from Robert's arms and took him away in the car.

"Follow them!" Cyril cried. "Stop, kidnappers!"

The children ran and ran. Finally, they spotted the sports car in the driveway of a mansion. They climbed over the fence,

then peeked in the windows and saw The Lamb sitting up at the table, having a feast of cookies, cakes and chocolates. He waved at them with his sticky fingers.

The window was open a little at the bottom, so Cyril boosted Jane up, and she squeezed through into the mansion. She scooped The Lamb up out of the chair and carried him back to the window. He began crying. "More cookies... no, Jane..."

As they raced down the road, they came upon a little girl. "What are you doing with my doll?" she demanded, grabbing onto one of The Lamb's feet. "Give him back to me."

"Oh, no. You must be mistaken," Anthea said. "This is not your doll. He is our baby brother."

The Lamb grinned and waved goodbye to the girl.

They continued walking. "Let's rest in that park for a while," Robert said. "I'm very hot and thirsty. Maybe there's a fountain there."

Jane's stomach growled. "We've missed lunch again."

They filled up on water, then sat down in the shade and soon fell asleep. Anthea woke up when she heard somebody say, "Goodness, look at the baby, Charlie. Let's take him for our very own."

A tall skinny man and a tall skinny lady were carrying The Lamb down a path into the woods. "Stop!" Anthea shouted. She jumped up and turned to the others. "We have to get him back!"

"What's going on? Why does everyone want to take our little Lamb?" Jane cried.

"Oh, no!" Robert said. "It was me. I wished somebody would want him..."

The four children chased the couple to a clearing in the woods where several tents were set up. Charlie and The Lamb sat out front of one of them.

"Excuse me, sir," Anthea said. "But that is our baby brother, and we need to take him home now."

"Excuse ME, miss," Charlie said. "Finders are keepers. I found this sweet little fellow, and Maggie and I are keeping him."

"Then there are a few things you should know about him," Jane said.

"Yes." Robert sat down on the ground. "He needs his diaper changed at least once every hour."

"And he only drinks milk that is warmed to exactly 68 degrees," Cyril said. "Do you have a thermometer and a microwave?"

The children watched the sky as their list of rules about The Lamb grew.

"And he gets very cross if you don't feed him chocolates at least ten times a day," Anthea said, just as the sky was turning orange and red.

"Well, he's very cute, but it sounds like he's hard to look after," Charlie said, passing the baby back to Cyril. "And he doesn't smell very good."

Robert grabbed his baby brother, and the children ran back to the white house.

"You missed lunch again – I made broccoli soup – you'll just have to have it tomorrow!" Martha said. "Wash up now! And get ready for supper. Peeuuu! When's the last time my precious had his diaper changed?"

While they were washing their hands, Jane said, "The Lamb is very cute, isn't he?"

"And he's funny," Robert said.

"Our family would be boring without him," Cyril admitted.

"We really must be more careful what we wish for next time," Anthea said.

CHAPTER 5

A Bird's Eye View of the World

In the morning, Anthea woke up before the others and tiptoed downstairs, then outside. She found the Sand Fairy curled up in a little ball in the sand pit. "Oh, are you not feeling well?" she asked. She scratched him behind the ears, and he crawled up onto her lap.

"I'm tired," he said. "And my whiskers are aching from the rain last night."

"Do you have arthritis, like Martha?" Anthea asked.

The Psammead shrugged. "They just hurt when they get wet."

She patted his head. "I wonder... um... would it be silly to wish for wings?"

He stared at her. "Why would that be silly? I would love to have wings."

She smiled. "Maybe you could come flying with us, then."

The Sand Fairy shook his head. "I must stay here. Besides, you might run into a rainstorm up there in the sky."

"Okay," Anthea said. "I have to go back home and ask the others first. Bye-bye!"

The other children were eating breakfast when she arrived at the house. "I would like to wish for wings," Anthea said. "What do you think?"

"Oh, yes," Cyril said. "I've always wanted to fly."

"Just think of all the things we could see," Robert said.

"Will they be pretty?" Jane asked.

Anthea smiled and nodded. "But we must go back and see the Sand Fairy first."

After Anthea had made her wish, the Sand Fairy did his

balloon trick, then disappeared into the ground.

"Feels like I've got pins and needles in my shoulders," Jane said, wiggling.

"Scratch my back, please, Anthea," Cyril said.

Anthea gasped. "Oh, oh – they're so beautiful!"

The children spread their arms to show each other their wings. Cyril's were as black as a raven's. Robert's were the blue of a blue jay. Anthea's were as white as a dove's, and Jane's were pale pink and lacy, like fairy wings.

"But can we really fly?" Cyril asked. He ran to the top of the sand pit, then jumped over the edge. He wobbled a bit at first, but then took off, straight up into the blue sky. The other children quickly followed him.

"Everything's so small!" Jane shouted.

"The whole world looks like a painting from up here," Anthea said.

"Woohooo!" screamed Cyril as he swooped past the others.

"Finally something good has come out of a wish. This is awesome!"

"It's hard work, though," Jane said, struggling to keep flapping her wings.

"I'm hungry," Robert complained after a while. "Let's go home."

"For broccoli soup? Eeeu!" said Anthea.

"You're right! I'd much rather have a nice hamburger. I still have my allowance – let's go and have a burger," Cyril said.

"And French fries!" Jane licked her lips.

The four children flew to the next town and coasted down onto the sidewalk. To their surprise, no one noticed their wings. "We're the only ones who can see them," Anthea said. "Cool!"

"I'm stuffed," Robert said, after finishing his second burger.

"There's a nice grassy hill," Cyril said. "Let's relax for a bit before we fly home."

"I love my fairy wings," Jane said. "But I'm a very sleepy fairy."

In just a few minutes, all four children were sound asleep.

Anthea shivered as she woke up. "What happened to the sun? Oh, no!" she cried, feeling her shoulders. "They're gone - my beautiful wings!"

"But, how will we get home now?" Robert asked. "We flew for miles and miles."

"We'll just take the subway," Cyril said, looking around.

Anthea rolled her eyes at him. "We're in the country, don't you remember? No buses, no subways, not even any trains."

Just then, a farmer driving a tractor with an empty wagon drove past.

"Wait!" Cyril shouted. "Wait for us!"

The farmer stopped, and the four children climbed up into the wagon.

"Yuck!" Jane whispered, plugging her nose. "I think he's a pig farmer."

"Well, it's better than walking," Anthea said.

When they got home, Martha was waiting by the front door.

"Peuuu! You smell awful! Where have you been? Just wait until your mother gets home," she added before any of the children could reply. "I've never seen such bad behavior from you children. Now get cleaned up and come for supper. Your broccoli soup is waiting!"

"We're sorry," Anthea said.

"Too late for that. And don't even ask to go exploring again tomorrow," Martha said. "You're all grounded!"

CHAPTER **6**

Castle Under Attack!

" **C** ould I please go outside, just for a few minutes to water the garden?" Robert begged at lunchtime the next day.

Martha looked at her watch. "For only 30 minutes – not one minute longer!"

Robert ran directly to the sand pit as soon as he got outside. Along the way, he tried to think of something good to wish for, but all he could think of were easy things like a new hockey stick or that Martha would make chocolate cake for dessert.

The Sand Fairy was out sunning himself on a big rock.

"What do you want?" he asked grumpily.

"Well, I was wondering if it's possible for one of the others to have their wish without having to come here to ask you," Robert said. "I can't think of anything good."

The Sand Fairy rolled over onto his belly. "Well, I suppose so. Now go away!"

As Robert walked up the lane, he stopped and stared. Where the white house had once been, there stood an enormous stone castle. There was no sign of the other children, but the castle was surrounded by marching soldiers carrying swords and crossbows and arrows.

The soldiers did not look friendly. Robert turned around and ran back to the sand pit. The Sand Fairy was fast asleep on the rock. "Pssst!" Robert whispered. "I need another wish. Fast. Please, Sand Fairy. I wish to be back with the others in the castle."

"Humph! If you must! But then leave me alone!" The Psammead puffed up, then turned over, and went back to sleep.

"Oh, Robert," Anthea said. "Thank goodness you're back. We're about to be attacked by those soldiers!"

"I don't like this game," Jane cried. "Why did Cyril have to wish for a war game?"

"Just like those horrible games you're always playing on the computer, Cyril," Anthea said. "And how did the Sand Fairy know about your wish?"

"Well..." Robert hesitated. "I asked the Psammead if we could have our wishes granted wherever we were – without us having to go down to see him every time. I guess he granted Cyril's wish right after I asked him."

"Too late to be mad, now," Cyril said. "Get to work. We've got to defend ourselves."

The castle was full of crossbows and swords that were too heavy for the children to lift. There were also lots of stones and plenty of water. The children piled the stones up on the windowsills and filled all the buckets they could find with water.

"But, I'm too hungry for a battle," Robert said.

"There's no food. We already looked," Anthea said.

"But, look at Martha. She's moving her arms like she's making pizza, but I can't see the pizza," Robert said.

"Remember? She doesn't see anything to do with the spells. She's just having her regular life," Anthea said.

Before Robert could answer, they all heard a loud blast from a trumpet.

"I see a soldier swimming across the moat!" Jane exclaimed.

A few seconds later, they heard a great crash, and the drawbridge fell across the moat. Horses thundered across the drawbridge and the soldiers began running around outside the castle walls.

"I'm scared!" Jane curled up in a corner and began to cry.

"They've got a cannon!" Cyril shouted.

As they watched, two of the soldiers wheeled the cannon across the drawbridge.

"They're aiming it straight up at us!" Robert yelled.

As they watched, the soldiers loaded three balls into the cannon, then prepared to light the fuse.

"Quick! Get some water – we have to put out the fuse," Robert called.

Anthea grabbed a bucket of water and passed it to Robert.

Robert dumped the first bucket of water on top of the cannon.

Cyril looked out the window that faced west. Only a thin sliver of the sun remained. Then it disappeared. The white house returned to normal.

"You think that's funny, do you?" Martha stomped into the room. "Dumping a bucket of water on your poor old housekeeper. It'll be bread and water instead of pizza for you children!"

CHAPTER **7**

Count Dracula Visits the Dentist

"**Y**ou should read this book after I'm finished, Anthea," Cyril said the next morning. "I wish I could meet Count Dracula."

Anthea put her hand over Cyril's mouth, but it was too late. She shivered and looked around at the others. They were standing in what looked like a castle dungeon. The room was dark, except for the light from the full moon. *How can that be? Wasn't it just morning?*

"Why is it dark?" Anthea asked.

"Dracula only comes out at night," Cyril said.

"But how will we know when the wish is almost finished?" Jane asked. "The sun already went down... I... I'm scared." Jane clung to her big sister's hand. "Is that a giant bat?"

"Good e... e... evening."

The children all spun around. "Count Dracula?" Cyril said.

The man nodded. "Indeed. Welcome to my castle. I hope you will enjoy your stay. Allow me to show you to your rooms."

"I'm not sleeping in a coffin," Cyril whispered.

"Could I interest you in something to drink?" Dracula asked, licking his red lips. "Some tomato juice, perhaps?"

Cyril buttoned his shirt collar up around his neck. The others did the same. From somewhere in the distance, a wolf howled.

"Is that a werewolf?" Jane asked, trembling. She edged into a corner. She screamed when something sticky touched her face. She pulled at it, then screamed again as a big hairy spider crawled across her nose.

Cyril reached out and flicked the hairy spider across the room.

"Wow! You're fast," Anthea said.

Cyril wiggled his fingers in the air. "Maybe all that time playing computer games wasn't wasted after all!"

"Now, about that drink!" Dracula said. "I'm getting thirsty!"

"Look at his teeth," Anthea whispered to Robert. "If our wishes usually disappear at sunset, maybe we will have to wait until sunrise for this wish to end. We won't survive a whole night with Dracula!"

Robert nodded. "We have to do something," he whispered back. After a few minutes, he clapped his hands. "I've got it! He needs to go to the dentist!"

Anthea grinned, then turned to face Dracula. "Excuse me, sir," she said. "I couldn't help but notice that your teeth are quite... um quite extraordinary." She looked at Robert and Cyril. "We have a friend, Dr... um... Dr. Incisor, who would be most interested in looking at your teeth."

Dracula opened his mouth wide so the children could see all of his long, white teeth. "I am very proud of my teeth –

they keep me alive, you might say. Let's go."

Cyril ran out ahead of the others. He turned his shirt around so he was wearing it backwards. He found a pair of glasses and some screwdrivers in the hall, dug his Swiss Army knife out of his pocket, then went to the library to set up his office.

The others led Dracula to the library and sat him down on the big revolving office chair.

"Good evening, Count Dracula," Cyril said. "I am Dr. Incisor, and I think I can help you with your overbite."

"Overbite? What do you mean?" the Count asked.

"Don't worry. I'm a professional," Cyril said. "Now, close your eyes and open wide."

When he did, Robert grabbed a tennis ball and stuffed it into the Count's mouth. It was a perfect fit. Then Anthea and Cyril tied his arms to the revolving chair and spun him around.

Jane laughed and danced around. "He can't bite us, now!"

"Mmmmmph!" Dracula kicked his legs in the air and struggled to speak.

"Now all we have to do is wait until sunset... I mean sunrise," Anthea corrected herself.

The children stayed awake all night, hiding from the bats and spiders and spinning Dracula around in the chair. Just before dawn, they heard something scratching and howling outside the library door. "It's a werewolf!" Jane cried. "I know it is!"

Just then, the sun peeked over the horizon, and Dracula disappeared in a puff of smoke.

"Home, sweet home!" Jane said as the white house returned to normal.

"We all have to be more careful about wishing out loud," Anthea said. "Right, Cyril?"

Cyril nodded and grinned. "I promise."

CHAPTER 8

Goodbye to
the Sand Fairy

M artha was listening to the radio when the children
came down for breakfast the next morning. "Good

heavens! Mrs. Ruby Vandergold has had all her jewelry stolen!

Bracelets, brooches, necklaces, even her diamond tiara."

"Oh, I wish Mom could have jewelry just like Mrs.

Vandergold's," Jane said.

Anthea laid her head down on the table. "Oh, no," she

groaned.

Sure enough, when they opened the door to their mother's

room, everything sparkled. Anthea picked up a heavy gold

bracelet and read the initials inside it. "RV," she said.

"Oh no! Mom's coming home today," Robert said. "The police will think she stole this stuff."

"What can we do with it?" Anthea said. "We can't just pack it all up and return it to Mrs. Vandergold."

"Let's go visit the Sand Fairy," Jane suggested.

As they walked out of the house, they saw their mother's car driving up the road.

"Hello, hello, children!" Mom said, giving each of them a hug. "And where's my little Lamb?"

Martha came outside carrying The Lamb.

"And have you all been good while I was away?" Mom asked.

Martha rolled her eyes as the children all nodded their heads.

"Now, let me just take my suitcase up to my room, and I'll be back down for a hot cup of tea. You can tell me all about your adventures."

Mom gasped as soon as she opened the door. "What's all this? Has the Queen been to visit while I was away?"

Cyril shrugged. "We don't know where it came from, but I do know Mrs. Vandergold had all her jewelry stolen last night."

"Well, I must go straight to the police, then," Mom said. "Help me gather up all these beautiful things."

"But the police will think Mom stole the jewelry," Jane whispered to Anthea.

"Now, Cyril – you stay here and guard these valuables while I'm gone," Mom said. "I'll be right back, with the police."

"As soon as she leaves, we'll go straight to the Sand Fairy," Anthea whispered to Jane.

And they did. He was curled up in a ball having a nap. "Well, what is it now? I'm getting a little tired of all your foolish wishes. I just might bite you!"

"Oh, please don't. This is very important," Jane said. "It's about our mother."

The Psammead smiled. "Oh – well, if it's about your mother, then let's hear it. I love mothers!"

Anthea explained the situation. "So what we'd really like is two things. First of all, I wish that Mom would never get to the police station and that she'd forget all about the jewelry."

"And second," Jane said. "I wish that Mrs. Vandergold would find out that her jewelry was never stolen."

The Sand Fairy blew himself up, bigger than ever before. Then he collapsed back to the ground. "Now, please let me sleep. I'm not as young as I used to be."

"Thank you!" The girls ran up the path to the house, just in time to see Mom's car turning into the driveway.

"Imagine! I got halfway to town, then I couldn't remember why I was going to town," Mom said.

Anthea shrugged. "Oh, well."

When they got in the house, Martha came to the door. "I just heard the news!" she announced, holding up her portable radio. "Mrs. Vandergold's maid had taken her jewelry out to be appraised and forgot to tell her. It wasn't stolen after all."

"Well, thank goodness for that," Mom said. "Now, how about a nice hot cup of tea?"

After tea, the children went back to the sand pit. The Psammead seemed to be waiting for them.

"Finally, it's my turn for a wish," he said.

"Well, that seems fair," Cyril said.

The Sand Fairy frowned at him. "My wish is that you will never tell anybody else about me. I'm too old and tired for much more wishing. Just think of the trouble it would cause if adults knew about me. They'd expect me to solve all their problems. The whole world would be turned topsy-turvy!"

Each of the children held up their right hand. "I solemnly promise never to tell anybody about the Psammead."

"But... could I just have one last, little, teeny, tiny wish?" Jane whispered into the Sand Fairy's hairy ear.

"Is it very, very small?" he asked.

She nodded.

"Very well, then."

"I wish that we will see you again, someday," she said.

The Psammead closed his eyes, blew himself up, his snail eyes spun in circles and his ears twitched. When he was back to normal, he said, "Then, you shall. Now, goodbye!"

But telling you, dear readers, where and when - now that would be a whole different story!